W9-AEO-164

The Smash-up Crash-up Derby

by Tres Seymour • pictures by S. D. Schindler

ORCHARD BOOKS • NEW YORK

JEFFERSONVILLE TOWNSHIP PUBLIC LIBRARY
JEFFERSONVILLE, INDIANA JUN 1995

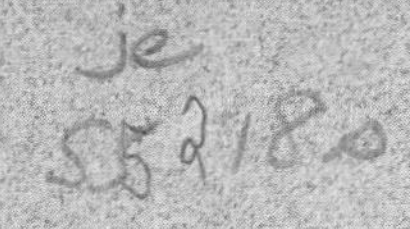

Text copyright © 1995 by Tres Seymour
Illustrations copyright © 1995 by S. D. Schindler
All rights reserved. No part of this book may be reproduced or transmitted in any form or by any means, electronic or mechanical, including photocopying, recording, or by any information storage or retrieval system, without permission in writing from the Publisher.

Orchard Books
95 Madison Avenue
New York, NY 10016

Manufactured in the United States of America
Printed by Barton Press, Inc.
Bound by Horowitz/Rae
Book design by Rosanne Kakos-Main

10 9 8 7 6 5 4 3 2 1

The text of this book is set in 16 point Eras Medium.
The illustrations are rendered in gouache and reproduced in full color.

Library of Congress Cataloging-in-Publication Data

Seymour, Tres.
The smash-up crash-up derby/by Tres Seymour;
pictures by S. D. Schindler.
p. cm.
"A Richard Jackson book"—Half t.p.
Summary: While visiting the fair, a child describes the most exciting event—the demolition derby and its surprise winner. ISBN 0-531-06881-1.—ISBN 0-531-08731-X (lib. bdg.) [1. Automobile racing—Fiction. 2. Fairs—Fiction. 3. Stories in rhyme.] I. Schindler, S. D., ill. II. Title.
PZ8.3.S496Sm 1995
[E]—dc20 94-24857

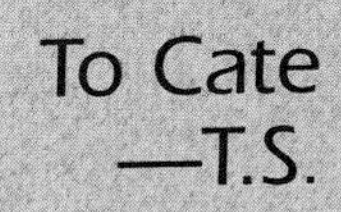

To Cate
—T.S.

It's September, and we've all come to the fair—
Mom and me, and Uncle Jake, and Aunt Marie.
We ride the Tilt-A-Whirl and we ride the carousel
And we throw darts at balloons to win a prize.
We don't win—

But that's not why we're here.

DART-O-R

CK

Never mind the cotton candy,
Never mind the livestock show,
Never mind the Ferris wheel,
There's just one place *we* want to go—

To the smash-up derby,
To the crash-up derby,
To the Demolition Derby at the fair!

DEMOLITION
DERBY
SATURDAY, SEPT. 27 - 3 P.M.
RJB

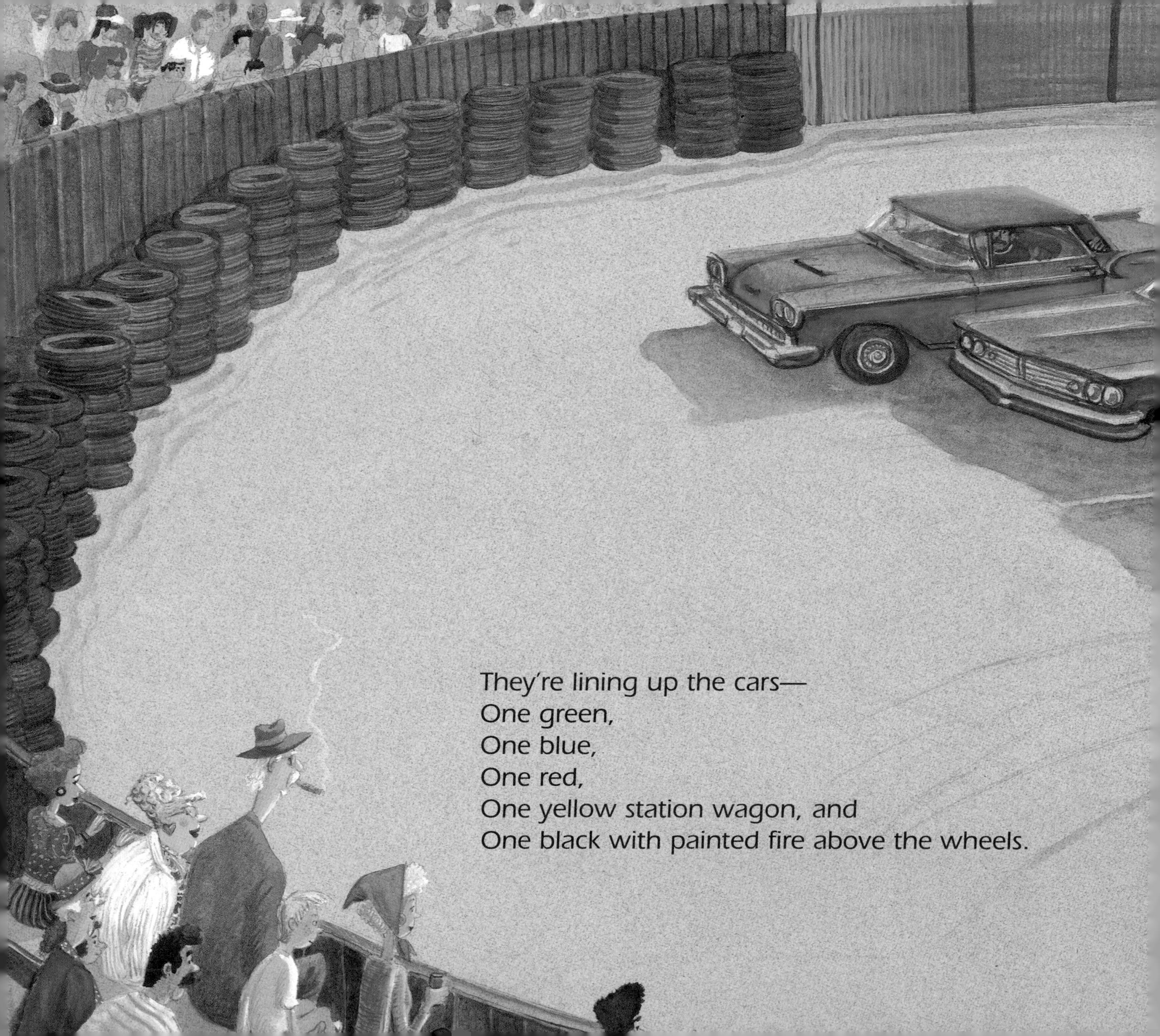

They're lining up the cars—
One green,
One blue,
One red,
One yellow station wagon, and
One black with painted fire above the wheels.

They start the cars, the green flags wave, they're off!
I clap, Aunt shouts, Mom squeals!
With the excitement of it all.
The fun about the derby is the
WHACK and *SCREECH* and
WHUMP and *HISS* and
THUMP and *POP* and
BANG

Until there's only one car left that runs.

I can see myself behind the wheel
Of a Mean Machine
With 13 painted on the side.
I'd put it into gear and ride
Like mad, to
WHACK!
WHUMP!
THUMP!

We're rooting for the yellow station wagon.
The driver's very quick
And makes his wheels go
SCRRREEEEEEECH!
Before he hits the blue car with a
BANG!

U-R-NEXT

The green car hits the red car
And the black car with the flame
Crumples up the blue car's bumper.
It will never look the same.

The cars all mingle in the ring.
They thrash and clash and groan and roar
Like dinosaurs
A zillion years ago.

The red car's stopped, and now the blue.
The green car's race is also through.

We see the black still running—Boo!

Now we see the station wagon and
We all stand up and cheer!

Except for Uncle Jake,
Who cannot bear to look, or hear.

The black car makes a running dash
To smash
The station wagon's side.
We hold our breath—

We see him miss!

The yellow station wagon hits
The black car with the fire above the wheels.

We hear an awful *POP* and *HISS!*

Aunt Marie lets out a shout!
The black car's stopped!
The black car's out!

What a grand old derby day!
It's the best we've ever had.
And now here comes the winner—
DAD!

Oh, there's nothing like the derby,
The smash-up, crash-up derby,
The Demolition Derby at the fair!